GOLDEN RULES FOR BEAUTIFUL LIFE

MY LUCKY ME

RUBEENA MOHAMMED

ISBN 979-888569931-0

I dedicate this book to My Parents.

Contents

Contents

Foreword

Everyone gets a little down in the tough times of life. Turn to reading this beautiful eperiences of this book, it will surely help you out to come out of the diffulties that you are facing .

Rubeena Mohammed

CHAPTER ONE

I'M BORN TO SMILE 24X7

I as an author, of this book love to express my gratitude to the time which helped me learn the importance of SMILE. There I examined myself that even after I dress up neatly, I look incomplete without wearing a SMILE on my FACE.

So far, I have experienced various definitions of SMILES, like it acts as a medicine in your illness, a support to your upliftment, mood changer, success mantra, secret to success in life.

Here, I remember a short story like to share with you all, there was a small girl who had some problem in her kidneys due to which she could not grow with all her other body parts and looks like a small baby doll 5years old.

She has actually participated on to the stage show to present her singing skills in Indian Idol and this is the real story, when she entered the hall of auditions of Indian Idol, wearing a big smile on her face despite of so many problems, struggles in her life it was not visible on her face, gave not only me but many others in the hall including judges, such a great inspiration for me and everyone else there, i,e; big lesson that LIFE is different for everyone, in various aspects and you cannot judge anyone with their looks, how a person is, I would like to quote the famous quote here " A book cannot be judged by its cover".

Today, I notice myself God has given me various reasons to smile, laugh, and be grateful for everything in LIFE.

Thank You, Thank You, Thank You

I love my beautiful SMILE.

Keep Smiling ?

On a mission to add SMILEs in people's life.

Your only job in this world is to SMILE 24x7.

Keep Smiling

CHAPTER TWO

I'M BORN TO SPREAD LAUGHTER & LOVE EVERYWHERE I GO.

I remembered the tough times of my life, that has taken away all beauties, laughter and love around me. The moment I realize that until I laugh and love myself nobody is bothered to do it for me. Become self-lover, nurture and pamper your own company. Then, the World out there waiting to see you lovely.

Thereafter, every time life gives me any types of situations in LIFE, I remember myself that my only JOB in this world is to lead a Joyful, Peaceful, Happiest & Healthiest Life in this WORLD and HEREAFTER.

Let me share an experience of this with you, When I felt sick I was sorrow about my ill-health I was worried and often fall sick, but once in my sickness I was watching the comedy show made me laugh, giggle so much which boosted every cell of my body recharged and felt energetic and experienced recovery.

"Laughter is the best and cheapest medicine."

Laughter will help you look young and bring you a problem free life

CHAPTER THREE

I'M MY BEST FRIEND.

Today I can proudly say that I'm my best friend. I love my lovely me more than any materialistic things in this World.

I LOVE myself.

I'm the BEST.

GOD is always with me.

I can achieve all the things I desire easily.

From the very beginning I can say my childhood, life has given me various reasons to face challenges due to which I experienced many up's and down's common in my LIFE.

I have seen people coming and going in my life easily, the one's I LOVE or the one's I Don't LOVE.

Then once LIFE has taught me the importance of SELF-LOVE, PEACE of MIND, and then slowly I understood that I was simply giving importance to the outside WORLD rather my inside ME. I was completely ignorant of myself till then and learnt these

3 best words : I ever know is I, me and myself.

Enter Caption

CHAPTER FOUR

WE LIVE EVERYDAY & WE DIE ONLY ONCE

This sentence has changed the meaning of my life ever. The day I understood the meaning of true living, Miracles start happening in my life every day and night.

From there onwards I started thanking everyday of my life as a gift and like-wise, life started giving me various gifts in various aspects.

Now,

Every day of my life is a MIRACLE filled with numerous gifts.

"Start your day and night being grateful."

"Start your day and night being happy."

"Start your and night Peacefully."

Y.O.D.O(You Only Die Once)

CHAPTER FIVE

LIFE IS MIRACULOUSLY BEAUTIFUL

Life is a bicycle. To keep the balance you need to keep moving. All the up's and down's in life are common, even the ECG report states that "the zig-zag line is alive and a straight line is dead symbol".

So never expect anything in return from others, just live the present moment fully.

The term LIFE is a bicycle states that the moment you want to ride the bicycle you need to pedal and manage the breaks, just by looking at the bicycle standing far away will not help you enjoy the ride. Same to same you can beautify your life with all good experiences and good teachings and learning.

Today, I can proudly say that I'm the most beautiful child of my LIFE who taught me many things and me the BEST VERSION of myself.

"THANK YOU MY BEAUTIFUL LIFE". You helped me become a new ME every day.

I'm LUCKY.

I'm Charming.

I'm BEAUTFUL from inside and outside.

CHAPTER SIX

ALWAYS TAKE THE BABY STEPS TO REACH YOUR GOALS

A goal can be achieved easily by taking the baby steps, with a fixed action plan because without the action plan its just a WISH. Consistency is the key to all the success.

The moment you put a deadline to your DREAM it becomes a GOAL.SET a GOAL that makes you step out of BED every morning.

80% Plan + 20% Action=100% Goal Achieved

Actions in small modules of 20% each until the goal achieved.

Here are Rules for SMART GOALS

S-Specific (Clear & Well Defined)

M-Measurable (Can be valued Precisely)

A-Attainable (Possible to achieve)

R-Relevant (Aligned with personal LIFE)

T-Time Bound (Have a DEADLINE)

DREAM BIG SET GOALS AND TAKE ACTIONS

Make a List of goals today

CHAPTER SEVEN

Be your own Sunshine

You can only bring shine in your life than in other's life when you have enough of your light that can spread around.

Just look at the SUN, it contains so much of light and heat in itself that's spreading sunshine around.

A Bright sunny day spreads more bright light than a dull cloudy day.

"Become your own master piece", you need to become more brighter if you want to shine and with your light the surroundings automatically gets brighter.

When LIFE gets CLOUDS create your own SUNSHINE.

CHAPTER EIGHT

HAPPINESS IS A FEELING THAT BRINGS MORE VALUE TO YOUR LIVING

My dear life was not less than the crest's and trough's of an ocean. But, once I realized to live a life feeling happy. That day the meaning of happy life came into my life, until then I used to complaint about my life.

Thank you my dear zindagi for giving me the taste of happiness in LIFE....

There onwards happiness, joyousness, beautiful, miraculous LIFE has become. Filled with excitement and small and big gifts in my LIFE.

Live every moment of your life joyfully.

Happiest Ever

CHAPTER NINE

BE GRATEFUL FOR EVERY SMALL OR BIG BLESSING IN YOUR LIFE

I started thanking My Almighty for each and every blessing in my life. The day I understood the meaning of grateful, gratitude, thankfulness.

- **Start counting your blessings, it will reverse your frustration and sorrow into blessings.**
- **Be thankful for all the gifts of your life, you will stop comparing yourself to anybody else in this world.**
- **Everyday you wake up, be thankful to Almighty for giving you another chance to fill happiness in your's & other's life.**

- **The act of gratitude may bring many other gifts of your LIFE filled with great good news.**

Here is a small gift for you all. Practice it every day in your LIFE to start MIRACLES.....

Stay Happy

CHAPTER TEN

YOU ARE A BEAUTIFUL CHARM & A BEAUTIFUL SOUL.

The moment I realized that God has created me for some special purpose. That day onwards I started giving importance to myself than any other Bollywood stars. That day, I defined the true meaning of LIFE.

There onwards ***I'm my own beauty Charm, my own beauty Princess and my own beauty Diva***. Even today I get best compliments from people that I look like a 16yrs college girl. So beautiful, Young and Dynamic.

Though I'm writing my very first LIFE experience book in my mid 20's. Thank you my lovely soul.

A beautiful Soul :
Loves without condition,
Talks without bad intention,
Gives without a reason.
And most of all
Cares for people
Without any expectation!!

CHAPTER ELEVEN

SUCCESS IS A JOURNEY NOT A DESTINATION

Those days when I use to come across failures was the biggest days of my life. I used to be broken, tampered, devastated, disappointed, depressed, unhappy, deadly broken, unlucky, ugly, etc all the terms that can define failure.

But slowly life has been my best teacher it taught me beautifully, that to feel the brightness ‘a dark room will help you better to understand the presence of brightness’.

“In order to be the light to shine so brightly, the darkness must be present.”

You will never the taste of SUCCESS without FAILURE it’s partner.

CHAPTER TWELVE

TIME IS BIGGEST RESOURCE OF MY LIFE

Unless and until I realized the importance of time, I was wasting it without any limits. Once I learnt the term TIME and its importance started using it resourcefully.

Today more than anything I Value TIME by just saying 2 simple words "THANK YOU" for all the good and bad timings of my LIFE.

Measure your time, because once the time flies it will never be back.

The 4 Ds of Time Management

Category	Action	Examples
Do	Work on tasks that only take a few minutes to complete. Quickly accomplishing a series of smaller tasks builds momentum for working on larger projects.	• Answering an email • Returning a phone call • Printing a report
Defer (Delay)	Temporarily pause a task that doesn't need to be handled right away, and schedule when you have the availability.	• New request from a colleague • New project idea
Delegate	Reassign an essential task to someone else.	• Weigh tasks that benefit from your specific expertise vs. those tasks that deliver the same outcome regardless of who is doing it
Delete (Drop)	Remove unnecessary tasks from your schedule and move on.	• Unproductive meetings • Unnecessary email

CHAPTER THIRTEEN

LIFE IS A BOOK

My most beautiful life, upon which I can write another book. Thank you for being so generous to me. People has used me badly for my generosity and kindness. Thank you my beautiful teacher(LIFE), in your guidance and presence I'm able to show case my important life to the World today.

You are the author of your book

Thank you for lovely gift i,e; my LIFE.

LIFE is like a book, don't jump to the end to see if it's WORTH it. Just enjoy life and fill the pages with beautiful & amazing memories.

CHAPTER FOURTEEN

ALWAYS KEEP THE CHILD INSIDE YOU ALIVE

Never let your age extinguish your inner child. This is the only thing which makes you happy from your heart.

Though I behave matured in front of people as per my situations, I'm childish inside, my inner peace, soul helps me to grow which adds taste of living alive.

Maturity comes from experiences and not from the age.

"Be Matured like a WOMEN

Be Childish like a KID"

Caring your inner child has a powerful & surprisingly quick results: Do it & let the child HEALS.

By connecting your inner child to your internal being, you bring out the HERO in you that exist in each one of us.

NEVER lose the KID in YOU.

CHAPTER FIFTEEN

NATURE IS MY 2ND BEST FRIEND

When life has given me loneliness. I started making my new friends i,e; my trees, my birds, my flowers, my pets, my vehicles, my earth, my sky, my water, my air, my stars, my rivers, my fields, my grass, etc. All that is in the nature helped me to grow and taught me various aspects of my life.

Love Nature & Protect it

I love to play with the nature. Thank You beautiful nature around me.

Talk to the beautiful nature around you, You will feel blessed, relaxed, cozy, happy inside & out.

Today make nature as your 2nd BEST FRIEND spend TIME with it often.

CHAPTER SIXTEEN

THIS EARTH IS MY LOVELY PLANET

My lovely planet earth, you are my home, my complete World. I love to see you fully from EAST, WEST, NORTH, SOUTH. So far, I have visited the most beautiful sacred holy place *The Makkah & The Medina.*

Thank You for my beautiful visit to my most holy place *"The Ka'aba"*, I wish all my readers whoever wish to go to the beloved place, Almighty grant all your wishes to come true easily.

Beautiful Planet Earth

Take responsibility to LOVE, CARE & PROTECT MOTHER EARTH. It is alive and Happy we are safe to survive.

Take care of all the natural resources that are given to us free of cost.

CHAPTER SEVENTEEN

I LOVE MY ETHICS AND VALUES

I give the whole & sole credit to my beloved Parents here, who gave me so beautiful life filled with all ethical values. To my beautiful teachings of our holy book The Quran, The beautiful teachings of the last messenger of the Almighty Allah "Prophet Muhammed Peace be Upon Him".

Never disobey law's or ethics follow them irrespective of comparison, one day you will realize it's value.

Follow Ethics and Values in your Life

You see the good around, you feel the good around.

CHAPTER EIGHTEEN

HAVE SELF-BELIEVE AND SELF-CONFIDENCE TO SURVIVE IN THIS WORLD

Since my childhood, thanks to Almighty who gave me positive mindset. Today I'm able to survive in this WORLD, after so many falls also just because of an attitude of self-confidence and learning attitude.

Because in this WORLD of Selfishness, people are least bothered about you living or dead. So, start taking care of yourself first then the WORLD will follow you.

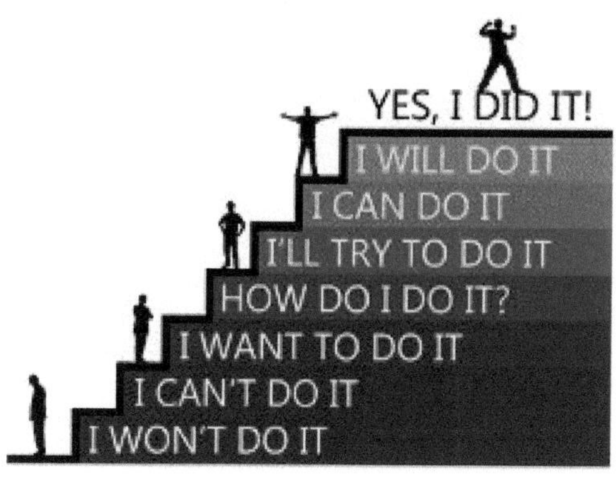

Your Success Ladder

Every day is a new beginning of self hope and happiness.

Develop self-Esteem and self-Confidence, it takes time to grow. And once it has grown it will never let you down.

Think Positively, Control Anger, Laugh often, be confident enough to deal all your aspects of life.

Ethics of Life

CHAPTER NINETEEN

YOU ARE BORN TO LEAD BY EXAMPLE

This attitude will help you develop the self-learning ability inside you. The only person who is concerned about you is first your parents next is the one you see in the mirror every day.

You can only LEAD by EXAMPLE if and only if you have Patience, Perseverance to excel and consistent towards all your actions which leads to achieve your goals.

Right from the very young age I was interested to look and watch the famous personalities of this WORLD like Thomas Alva Edison, Albert Einstein, Newton, Dr. A.P.J Abdul Kalam, etc.

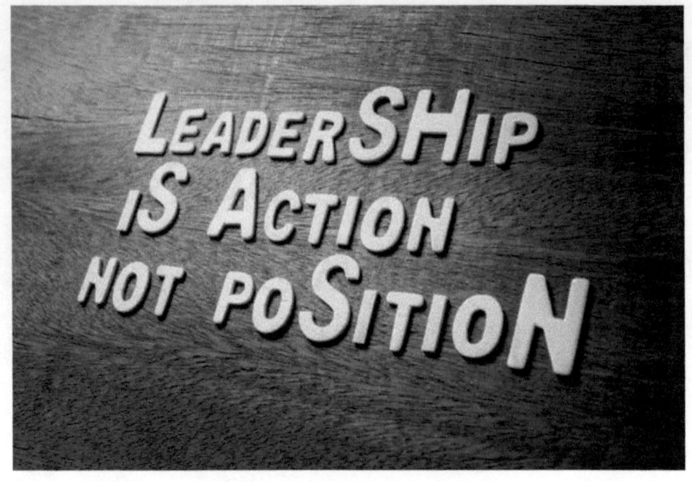

Leadership inside You

Today, I can guarantee I'm leading an Example just because of the foundational steps inside me to follow the path of the successful people of this World.

LEAD By

E-Every

X-eXcellent

A-Attitude

M-Mirrored

P-Positively

L-Lifts

E-Everyone

People may doubt what you say, But they will believe what you believe.

CHAPTER TWENTY

BE HUNGRY FOR ALL YOUR GOALS

If you want to be HAPPY set a GOAL that commands your thoughts, liberates your energy and inspires your HOPES.

Tie your knot to the GOALS and not to the expectations of the PEOPLE, that always hurts you.

LIFE is far more better when it is tied to GOALs rather than people who ruin your expectations.

BE Hungry for SUCCESS.

BE Hungry to make your MARK.

Hungry to be seen, to be heard & to have an effect.

And as you rise and become Successful, make sure also to be Hungry for Helping OTHER's.

Success Wheel

CHAPTER TWENTY-ONE

Always Take Calculated Risk

Thanks to Almighty that I have been always fighter in my journey of my life. Time to time I started taking RISK, few a times when failed I broke with huge losses without any experiences. Then, I realized the famous quote

Take Risk:

"if you Win, YOU WILL BE HAPPY"

"If you Lose, YOU WILL BE WISE".

Famous quote by Dhirubhai Ambani:

"You have to take calculated risk, to earn something ".

Example:

How to Calculate Risk

Risk = Probability of Loss x Value of Loss

Scenario: A local coffee shop purchases a 5-year-old espresso machine for $5,000 that has a 10% chance of breaking down in the next 12 months. The risk level can be quantified as $500 ($5,000 x 0.10).

Characteristics of a Calculated Risk-Taker

- Optimistic about all possibilities
- Comfortable taking chances
- Agile and able to adapt when there's ambiguity
- Focused on execution

Pinterest failed to generate a critical mass after its launch in 2010, so the founder and a few programmers ran the site out of a small apartment until the summer of 2011.

Charmin decided to use toilet humor to engage its audience in 2014. It's continued to enjoy marketing success with comic relief addressing an awkward topic.

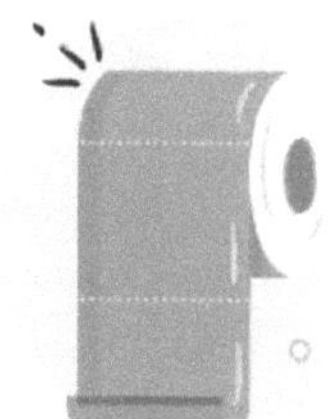

Steps to Taking Calculated Risks

Do your due diligence

- Don't base a decision on emotions. Instead, evaluate every detail.
- Ask advice from a trusted advisor and analyze the numbers.

Anticipate mistakes

- Discover red flags or potential issues before they occur. Ask probing questions:
  A. If a deal loses money, how will your business respond?
  B. If a partnership breaks down, what course of action will you take?
  C. If a project falls behind, how will you meet the deadline?

Set checkpoints

- Carefully identify and implement your goals.
- Set a specific date each month to assess your progress.

Jump when it feels right

Rely on your research and data, then take the plunge.

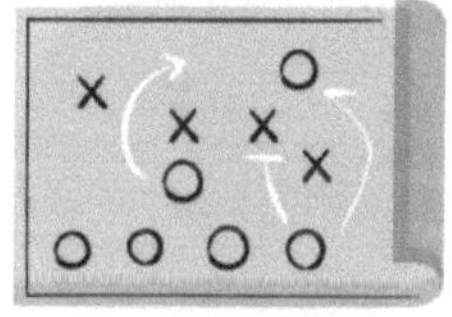

Be ready to pivot

Revise your plan of action if a budget gets cut or a partnership falls through.

CHAPTER TWENTY-TWO

SAY THIS TO YOURSELF EVERY MORNING

1. *I'm thankful and grateful for this day.*
2. *I'm the best and I deserve the best.*
3. *I'm happy and healthy.*
4. *I'm Successful in every area of my life.*
5. *I'm beautiful inside and outside.*
6. *I'm Prosperous.*
7. *I enjoy my Work.*
8. *I'm Wealthy.*
9. *I'm Loved.*
10. *I'm secure.*
11. *I'm forgiving*
12. *I'm forgiven.*
13. *I'm grateful.*
14. *I'm Confident*
15. *I'm attractive.*
16. *I'm Lucky*
17. *I'm Courageous*

18. *I'm excited about my day.*
19. *I believe in myself*
20. *I believe in Miracles every day & night.*
21. *I breathe in relaxation & I breathe out tension.*
22. *Today is my DAY.*
23. *I'm ready to receive the gifts of my LIFE.*
24. *I'm attracting positive energy into my life.*
25. *I'm calmer with each deep breathe I take.*

CHAPTER TWENTY-THREE

A GIFT TO ALL MY READERS DAY-1

JACK'S SCHOOL TO-DO'S

TO-DO LIST

•
•
•
•
•
•
•
•
•

NOTES

DAILY SCHEDULE

6 AM

7 AM

8 AM

9 AM

10 AM

11 AM

12 PM

1 PM

2 PM

3 PM

4 PM

5 PM

6 PM

Practice this Every Day

Day-2

JACK'S SCHOOL TO-DO'S

TO-DO LIST

-
-
-
-
-
-
-
-
-

NOTES

DAILY SCHEDULE

6AM

7AM

8AM

9 AM

10 AM

11 AM

12 PM

1PM

2 PM

3 PM

4 PM

5 PM

6 PM

Practice this Every Day

Day-3

JACK'S SCHOOL TO-DO'S

TO-DO LIST

-
-
-
-
-
-
-
-
-

NOTES

DAILY SCHEDULE

6 AM

7 AM

8 AM

9 AM

10 AM

11 AM

12 PM

1 PM

2 PM

3 PM

4 PM

5 PM

6 PM

Practice this Every Day

Day-4

JACK'S SCHOOL TO-DO'S

TO-DO LIST	DAILY SCHEDULE
•	6AM
•	7AM
•	8AM
•	9 AM
•	10 AM
•	11 AM
•	12 PM
•	1PM
•	2 PM
NOTES	3 PM
	4 PM
	5 PM
	6 PM

Practice this Every Day

Day-5

JACK'S SCHOOL TO-DO'S

TO-DO LIST

-
-
-
-
-
-
-
-
-

NOTES

DAILY SCHEDULE

6AM

7AM

8AM

9 AM

10 AM

11 AM

12 PM

1PM

2 PM

3 PM

4 PM

5 PM

6 PM

Practice this Every Day

Day-6

JACK'S SCHOOL TO-DO'S

TO-DO LIST

-
-
-
-
-
-
-
-
-

NOTES

DAILY SCHEDULE

6AM

7AM

8AM

9 AM

10 AM

11 AM

12 PM

1PM

2 PM

3 PM

4 PM

5 PM

6 PM

Practice this Every Day

Day-7

JACK'S SCHOOL TO-DO'S

TO-DO LIST

-
-
-
-
-
-
-
-
-

NOTES

DAILY SCHEDULE

6 AM

7 AM

8 AM

9 AM

10 AM

11 AM

12 PM

1 PM

2 PM

3 PM

4 PM

5 PM

6 PM

Practice this Every Day

Rubeena Mohammed

Rubeena Mohammed is an author, educator, business consultant, Software Trainer, Programmer, Coach.

A Dynamic Personality multi-talented and known as Youngest Inspirational Speaker changing the lifes of many by her teachings.

The author is young and dynamic who shares the various experiences of her life at the very young age. She expresses her views upon the life and its teachings, this way author wants to help her audience to overcome tough times of life. The author is also a dynamic professor in computer science.

9 798885 699310

Printed by Libri Plureos GmbH in Hamburg, Germany